# BABY'S BEST BOOK

WRITTEN BY **Tony Bradman**        ILLUSTRATED BY **Lisa Kopper**

Harper & Row, Publishers

Baby's Best Book
Text copyright © 1987 by Tony Bradman
Illustrations copyright © 1987 by Lisa Kopper
First published in Great Britain in 1987 by Methuen Children's Books Ltd
For information address Harper & Row Junior Books,
10 East 53rd Street, New York, N.Y. 10022.
1  2  3  4  5  6  7  8  9  10
First American Edition
Library of Congress Cataloging-in-Publication Data
Bradman, Tony.
Baby's best book.

    Summary: Presents a collection of nursery rhymes,
folk and fairy tales, simple games, and picture puzzles.
    1. Children's literature.   [1. Literature—
Collections.   2. Folklore.   3. Nursery rhymes]
I. Kopper, Lisa.   II. Title.
PZ5.B73Bab 1987      [E]      87-45275
ISBN 0-06-020716-7
ISBN 0-06-020717-5 (lib. bdg.)

# *Contents*

# Nursery Stories

## The Gingerbread Man

Once upon a time, there was an old woman who lived alone with her husband. One day, the old woman decided to make a gingerbread man for them both.

So she made a little figure out of gingerbread, and gave him currants for his eyes, raisins for the buttons on his coat, and a great big smile. And then she popped him in the oven to cook.

A little while later, the old woman and her husband heard a strange sound coming from the oven. It was a tiny little voice saying, "Let me out! Let me out!"

The old woman opened the oven door, and quick as a flash the little gingerbread man ran out of their house and away up the road. The old woman and her husband chased after him. "Come back!" they called.

But the little gingerbread man wouldn't come back. He ran and he ran and he ran, and he sang this song: "Run, run, as fast as you can, you can't catch me, I'm the gingerbread man!"

A cow saw the little gingerbread man running past, and said, "Come back! I'd like to eat you!" And the cow chased after him, followed by the old woman and her husband.

But the little gingerbread man wouldn't come back. He ran and he ran and he ran, and he sang this song: "Run, run, as fast as you can, you can't catch me, I'm the gingerbread man!"

Next, a horse saw the little gingerbread man running past, and said, "Come back! I'd like to eat you!" And the horse chased after him, followed by the cow, and the old woman and her husband.

But the little gingerbread man wouldn't come back. He ran and he ran and he ran, and he sang this song: "Run, run, as fast as you can, you can't catch me, I'm the gingerbread man!"

Then some men working by a river saw the little gingerbread man running past, and said, "Come back! We'd like to eat you!"

But the little gingerbread man wouldn't come back. He ran and he ran and he ran, and he sang this song: "Run, run, as fast as you can, you can't catch me, I'm the gingerbread man!" And the men chased after him, followed by the horse, and the cow, and the old woman and her husband.

None of them could catch him, but at last the little gingerbread man came to a river. He had to cross it, but he could not swim.

Now it so happened that a fox was sitting by the riverbank at that moment.

"Hop on my back," said the fox to the little gingerbread man. "I'll take you across and they won't catch you!"

So the little gingerbread man climbed on the fox's back, and they swam across the river. But when they got to the other side, the fox tossed the little gingerbread man as high as he could . . . then caught him and gobbled him up.

On the other side of the river, the men, the horse, the cow, and the old woman and her husband heard a little voice calling, "Let me out! Let me out!"

But it was too late.

# Little Red Riding Hood

Once upon a time, there was a girl who lived near a dark, dark wood. She had a lovely red cloak that she liked to wear all the time, and so everyone called her Little Red Riding Hood.

One day, Little Red Riding Hood's mother asked her to take a cake to her grandmother, who lived on the other side of the dark, dark wood.

Now deep in the heart of that dark, dark wood, there lived a big, bad wolf. That day, the big bad wolf was feeling very hungry. And just as he was wondering what to have for his dinner, who should he see . . . but Little Red Riding Hood!

The big bad wolf followed Little Red Riding Hood, and was just about to gobble her up when he saw a woodcutter looking at him. The woodcutter told Little Red Riding Hood to be careful in the wood, and asked her where she was going.

When the big bad wolf heard she was going to see her grandmother, he decided to play a trick on Little Red Riding Hood. He raced off to her grandmother's cottage, jumped in through a window, tied her up and hid her under the bed.

Then he put on the grandmother's clothes, got into the bed, and waited for Little Red Riding Hood.

When she got to the cottage, Little Red Riding Hood knocked on the door and went in.

"My, my, grandmother," she said. "You don't look well at all! And what big eyes you've got!"

"All the better to see you with," said the crafty wolf.

"And what big ears you've got," said Little Red Riding Hood.

"All the better to hear you with," said the nasty wolf.

"And what big teeth you've got!" said Little Red Riding Hood.

"All the better...to gobble you up with!" roared the big bad wolf. He leaped out of the bed, and was just about to gobble up poor Little Red Riding Hood...when the woodcutter came in through the door with his great big axe.

Well, the big bad wolf was so frightened that he jumped out of the window, and ran off howling into the dark, dark wood.

Little Red Riding Hood soon found her grandmother, and they both thanked the woodcutter.

And whenever she came to see her grandmother after that, Little Red Riding Hood was very, very careful and kept an eye out for trouble.

But the big bad wolf was never seen again.

# Goldilocks and the Three Bears

Once upon a time, there were three bears who lived in a cottage in the woods. There was a great big daddy bear, a medium-sized mommy bear, and a tiny little baby bear, and they were very happy.

One morning they had porridge for breakfast. But it was too hot, so they decided to go for a walk while it cooled down.

While they were out, a naughty little girl called Goldilocks came upon their cottage, and looked in through the window.

"What a lovely little cottage," she thought. She could see no one inside, so she opened the door and went in.

The first thing she saw was the breakfast table and the three bowls upon it. Goldilocks could smell the good, warm porridge, and just couldn't stop herself from trying some.

First she tasted the porridge in the great big bowl, but that was too hot. Then she tasted the porridge in the medium-sized bowl, but that was too cold. Last of all she tasted the porridge in the tiny little bowl, and that was just right – yummy yummy!

Then Goldilocks thought she'd like to sit down. First she sat in the great big chair, but that was too hard. Then she sat in the medium-sized chair, but that was too soft. Last of all she sat in the tiny little chair, and that was just right. But Goldilocks was too heavy for it . . . and all the legs broke off!

Goldilocks was beginning to feel tired, so she went upstairs to find somewhere to lie down. First she lay down on the great big bed, but that was too lumpy. Next she lay down on the medium-sized bed, but that had too many broken springs. Last of all she lay down on the tiny little bed, and that was just right. And soon Goldilocks was snoring away.

Not long after Goldilocks fell asleep upstairs, the three bears came home. They knew something was wrong right away.

"Who's been eating my porridge?" said the great big daddy bear in his loud voice.

"And who's been eating *my* porridge?" said the medium-sized mommy bear in her soft voice.

"And who's been eating my porridge . . . and gobbled it all up?" said the tiny little baby bear in his squeaky voice.

Then the three bears saw their chairs.

"Who's been sitting in my chair?" said the great big daddy bear in his loud voice.

"And who's been sitting in *my* chair?" said the medium-sized mommy bear in her soft voice.

"And who's been sitting in my chair ... and broken it all up?" said the tiny little baby bear in his squeaky voice.

Then the three bears went upstairs.

"Who's been sleeping in my bed?" said the great big daddy bear in his loud voice.

"And who's been sleeping in *my* bed?" said the medium-sized mommy bear in her soft voice.

The tiny little baby bear was jumping up and down.

"I know who's been sleeping in my bed," he said in his squeaky little voice. *"Because she's still there!"*

Just at that moment, Goldilocks woke up. She saw the three bears standing around her as she lay on the bed, and she was very scared by their angry faces. She knew she had been a bad, bad girl.

So she jumped up and ran down the stairs and she didn't stop running until she got home. That was the last time the three bears saw her. And although she didn't stop being naughty, she never did anything quite so bad again.

# The Three Billy Goats Gruff

Once upon a time, there were three billy goats by the name of Gruff. There was a baby billy goat, a middle billy goat, and a big billy goat, and they had eaten all the grass on one side of the river.

They wanted to cross the river to eat the nice, juicy green grass on the other side. But the only bridge was guarded by a mean and nasty troll whose favorite food was fresh, succulent . . . billy goat.

So the three billy goats came up with a plan, and this is what they did.

The first of the billy goats to cross the bridge was the baby billy goat Gruff. He went walking across, trip-trap, trip-trap, until he was stopped by the mean and nasty troll.

"Who's that trip-trapping over my bridge?" he roared, showing his great, sharp teeth.

"It's only me, the baby billy goat Gruff, and I'm going to eat the juicy grass on the other side of the river."

"Oh, no you're not," roared the mean and nasty troll, "because I'm going to GOBBLE YOU UP!"

"Oh, please don't do that," said the baby billy goat Gruff. "Wait for my brother, the middle billy goat Gruff. He's much bigger and tastier than I!"

The mean and nasty troll thought for a while.

"All right," he said at last. "Be off with you!"

The second of the billy goats to cross the bridge was the middle billy goat Gruff. He went walking across, trip-trap, trip-trap, until he was stopped by the mean and nasty troll.

"Who's that trip-trapping over my bridge?" he roared, showing his great, sharp teeth.

"It's only me, the middle billy goat Gruff, and I'm going to eat the juicy grass on the other side of the river."

"Oh, no you're not," roared the mean and nasty troll, "because I'm going to GOBBLE YOU UP!"

"Oh, please don't do that," said the middle billy goat Gruff. "Wait for my brother, the big billy goat Gruff. He's much bigger and tastier than I!"

The mean and nasty troll thought for a while.

"All right," he said at last. "Be off with you!"

The third of the billy goats to cross the bridge was the big billy goat Gruff. He went walking across, trip-trap, trip-trap, until he was stopped by the mean and nasty troll.

"Who's that trip-trapping over my bridge?" he roared, showing his great, sharp teeth.

"It's only me, the big billy goat Gruff, and I'm going to eat the juicy grass on the other side of the river."

"Oh, no you're not," roared the mean and nasty troll. But before he could say anything else, the big billy goat Gruff charged down the bridge towards him, clatter, clatter, clatter, and knocked him into the water, SPLASH!

"Oh, yes I am!" said the big billy goat Gruff.

And from then on, the three billy goats Gruff could cross the bridge and eat all the juicy grass whenever they wanted.

And the mean and nasty troll was never seen again.

# The Three Little Pigs

Once upon a time, there were three little pigs who wanted to leave home. They said good-bye to their mother and father, and each of them went off to build a house to live in.

The first little pig built his house of straw. The second little pig built his house of sticks. And the third little pig built his house of bricks, with a nice big chimney.

One day, the big bad wolf came up to the first little pig's house and knocked on the door, rat-a-tat-tat.

"Little pig, little pig," he growled, "let me come in!"

And inside his straw house, the little pig, whose knees were knock-knock-knocking together because he was so frightened, squealed back: "N-n-n-no, not by the hair of my chinny-chin-chin!"

"Well then," roared the big bad wolf, "I'll huff and I'll puff and I'll BLOW your house in!"

So he huffed and he puffed and he blew the house in, but the little pig ran off to hide in his brother's house of sticks.

The big bad wolf came up to the second little pig's house and knocked on the door, rat-a-tat-tat.

"Little pigs, little pigs," he snarled, "let me come in!"

And inside the stick house, the little pigs, whose knees were knock-knock-knocking together because they were so frightened, squealed back: "N-n-n-no, not by the hair of our chinny-chin-chins!"

"Well then," roared the big bad wolf, "I'll huff and I'll puff and I'll BLOW your house in!"

So he huffed and he puffed and he blew the house in, but the little pigs ran off to hide in their brother's house of bricks.

The big bad wolf came up to the third little pig's house and knocked on the door, rat-a-tat-tat.

"Little pigs, little pigs," he growled, "let me come in!"

And inside the brick house, the little pigs, whose knees were knock-knock-knocking together because they were so frightened, squealed back: "N-n-n-no, not by the hair of our chinny-chin-chins!"

"Well then," roared the wolf, "I'll huff and I'll puff and I'll BLOW your house in!"

So he huffed and he puffed, but he couldn't blow the brick house in. The big bad wolf was very angry, and thought that he would climb down the brick house's chimney to get at the three little pigs.

But on the fire at the bottom of the chimney was a great big pot of soup. Down came the big bad wolf into the pot . . . and burnt his bottom! With a roar he ran out of the house, huffing and puffing all the way, with smoke pouring from his tail.

And the three little pigs laughed so much they cried.

# Peek-a-boo Baby

# Hide
# and
# Seek
# Babies

There are ten babies
hiding in this picture.
Can you find them?

# Can You Make These Noises?

All these things make noises.
Can you make all these noises too?

trumpet

rooty toot toot! rooty toot toot!

drum

bang! bang!

dog

lion

roar! roar!

woof! woof!

snake     hissss! hissss!

telephone

drinngg! drinngg!

baby

wah! wah!

car

brrrmm! brrrmm!

Can you shout like this?

cat

meow! meow!

**a** is for apple

**b** is for boots

**c** is for car

**d** is for dad

**e** is for egg

**j** is for jumping

**k** is for kitten

**n** is for noisy

**l** is for love
**m** is for mom

**t** is for toys

**u** is for upset

**v** is for vase

22

**f** is for family

**g** is for grandparents

**h** is for happy

**i** is for ill

**o** is for orange

**q** is for quiet time

**r** is for riding
**s** is for sister

**p** is for painting

**x** is for kisses

**y** is for yummy yummy

**z** is for zzzz . . .

**w** is for wet

# Baby's A B C

23

# Baby's 1 2 3

**one** for the penny
     bright in my hand,

**two** for my bucket
and spade in the sand,

**three** for the wheels
  on my little trike,

**four** for the legs
of the chair that I like,

**five** for the buttons on my winter coat,

**six** for the sailors in my bath-time boat,

**seven** for the teddy bears
asleep in my bed,

**eight** for the
whiskers on
my kitten's head,

**nine** for the pictures
on my bedroom wall,

And **ten** for my fingers –
that's all!

# Baby's Holiday

I've been packing
For my holiday,
We're going
To the beach today;
A bucket and spade
For my holiday
Sun and sea and sand –
Hooray!

I'll start digging
To make a castle tall,
Build it up
To keep the sea away;
Here comes the sea
Knocking down the walls,
Sun and sea and sand –
Hooray!

Paddling and swimming
In the cold blue sea,
Splashing and diving,
All the day;
I'm so wet
And there's sand all over me,
Sun and sea and sand –
Hooray!

Time's gone fast
On our holiday,
We're going home
In our car today;
We've had fun
On our holiday,
Sun and sea and sand –
HOORAY!

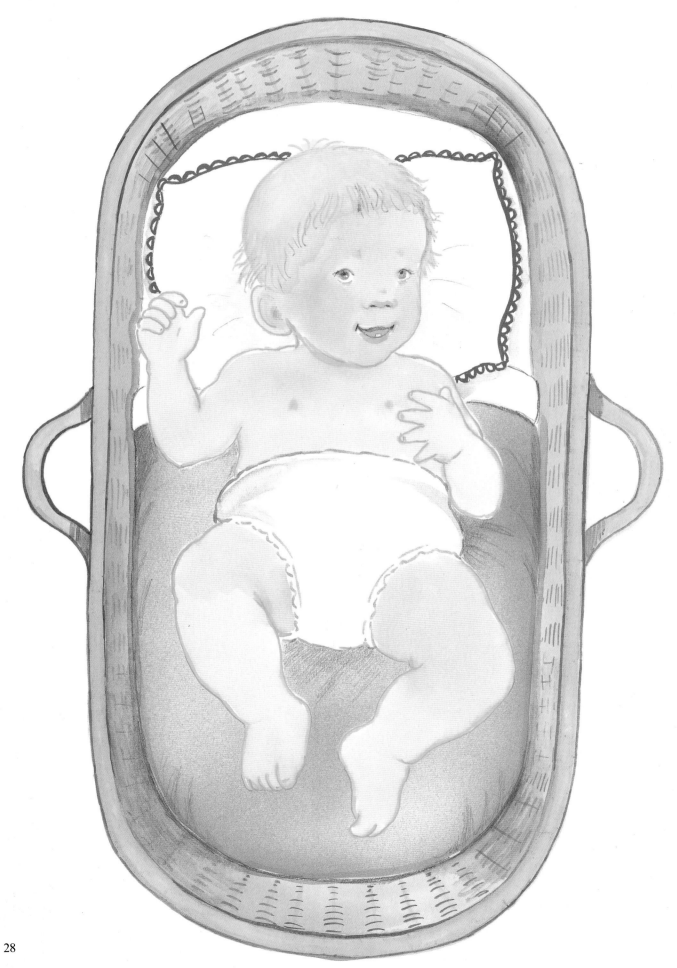

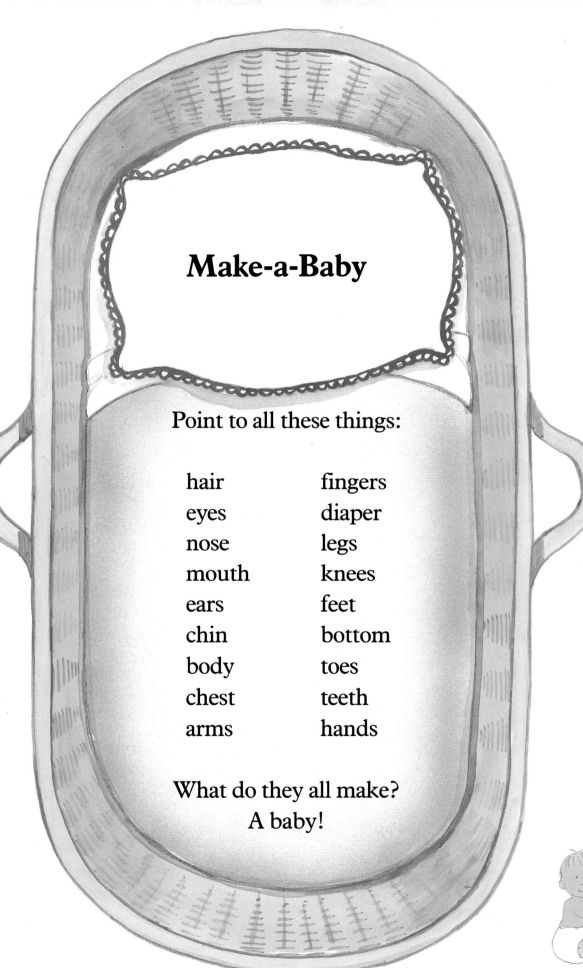

# Make-a-Baby

Point to all these things:

| | |
|---|---|
| hair | fingers |
| eyes | diaper |
| nose | legs |
| mouth | knees |
| ears | feet |
| chin | bottom |
| body | toes |
| chest | teeth |
| arms | hands |

What do they all make?
A baby!

# My Favorite Things

These are all my favorite things.
Can you find them in the picture?

| | |
|---|---|
| teddy bear | bottle |
| spoon | crayon |
| cup | paints |
| tricycle | potty |
| chair | diaper |
| bed | doll |
| toothbrush | jack-in-the-box |
| ball | stroller |
| books | bowl |

# Action Rhymes

### The Teapot

I'm a little teapot, short and stout.
Here's my handle,
Here's my spout.
When I am all steamed up, hear me shout –
Tip me over and pour me out!

### Pat-a-Cake

Pat-a-cake, pat-a-cake, baker's man,
Bake me a cake as fast as you can.
Pat it and prick it and mark it with a B . . .
And put it in the oven for Baby and me!

### Row, Row, Row Your Boat

Row, row, row your boat,
Gently down the stream,
Merrily, merrily, merrily, merrily,
Life is but a dream.

## Where Is Thumbkin?

Where is Thumbkin?
Where is Thumbkin?
Here I am, here I am.
How are you this morning?
Very well, I thank you.
Run away, run away.

Where is Pointer?
Where is Pointer?
Here I am, here I am.
How are you this morning?
Very well, I thank you.
Run away, run away.

Where is Tall Man?
Where is Tall Man?
Here I am, here I am.
How are you this morning?
Very well, I thank you.
Run away, run away.

Where is Ring Finger?
Where is Ring Finger?
Here I am, here I am.
How are you this morning?
Very well, I thank you.
Run away, run away.

Where is Pinky?
Where is Pinky?
Here I am, here I am.
How are you this morning?
Very well, I thank you.
Run away, run away.

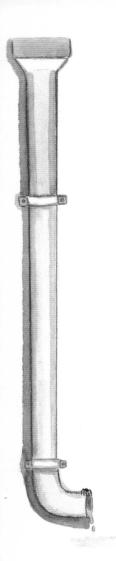

## The Incy Wincy Spider

The incy wincy spider
Climbed up the water spout.
Down came the rain,
And washed the spider out.
Out came the sun,
And dried up all the rain,
And the incy wincy spider
Climbed up the spout again.

## This Little Piggy

This little piggy went to market;
This little piggy stayed at home.
This little piggy had roast beef;
This little piggy had none.
And this little piggy cried,
Wee wee wee wee, all the way home!

## Ride a Cock-Horse

Ride a cock-horse,
    To Banbury Cross,
To see a fine lady
    Upon a white horse.
Rings on her fingers
    And bells on her toes,
She shall have music
    Wherever she goes.

## Two Little Dicky Birds

Two little dicky birds,
Sitting on a wall,
One named Peter,
One named Paul.

Fly away Peter!
Fly away Paul!
Come back Peter,
Come back Paul.

35

## Hickory Dickory Dock

Hickory, dickory, dock,
The mouse ran up the clock;
The clock struck one,
The mouse ran down,
Hickory, dickory, dock.

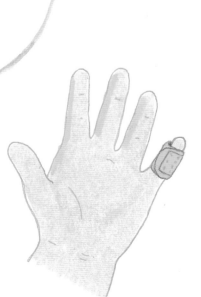

## One, Two, Three, Four, Five

One, two, three, four, five,
Once I caught a fish alive.
Six, seven, eight, nine, ten,
Then I let it go again.
Why did you let it go?
Because it bit my finger so.
Which finger did it bite?
This little finger on the right!

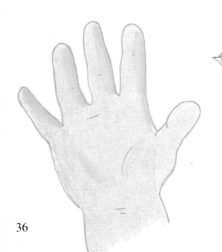

## Round and Round

Round and round the garden,
Runs the teddy bear.
One step, two steps,
Tickle you under there!

Round and round the haystack,
Runs the little mouse.
One step, two steps,
And in his little house!

Round and round the baby,
Run the mouse and teddy bear . . .
One step, two steps,
Tickle you everywhere!

# Nursery Rhymes

### Georgie-Porgie

Georgie-Porgie, pudding and pie,
Kissed the girls and made them cry;
When the boys came out to play,
Georgie-Porgie ran away.

### Mary, Mary

Mary, Mary, quite contrary,
   How does your garden grow?
With silver bells and cockle shells
   And pretty maids all in a row.

### Humpty Dumpty

Humpty Dumpty sat on a wall,
Humpty Dumpty had a great fall;
All the king's horses and all the king's men,
Couldn't put Humpty together again.

## My Son John

Diddle, diddle, dumpling, my son John,
Went to bed with his trousers on;
One shoe off and one shoe on,
Diddle, diddle, dumpling, my son John.

## Willie Winkie

Wee Willie Winkie runs through town,
Upstairs and downstairs in his nightgown,
Rapping at the window, crying through the lock,
Are the children all in bed, it's past eight o'clock?

## Tom

Tom, Tom, the piper's son,
Stole a pig and away did run;
    The pig was eat
    And Tom was beat,
And Tom went howling down the street.

## There Was an Old Woman

There was an old woman who lived in a shoe,
She had so many children she didn't know what to do;
She gave them some broth without any bread;
She whipped them all soundly and put them to bed.

## Little Bo Peep

Little Bo Peep
 Has lost her sheep
And doesn't know
 Where to find them;
Leave them alone
 And they'll come home
Bringing their tails
 Behind them.

## Tommy Tucker

Little Tommy Tucker
 Sings for his supper.
What shall we give him?
 White bread and butter.
How shall he cut it
 Without ever a knife?
How shall he marry
 Without ever a wife?

## Jack Horner

Little Jack Horner,
Sat in the corner,
Eating his Christmas pie;
He put in his thumb,
And pulled out a plum,
And said, What a good boy am I!

## Little Boy Blue

Little Boy Blue,
   Come blow your horn,
The sheep's in the meadow,
   The cow's in the corn.
Where is the boy
   Who looks after the sheep?
He's under a haystack
   Fast asleep.
Will you wake him?
   No, not I.
For if I do,
   He's sure to cry.

## Ding Dong Bell

Ding, dong, bell,
Pussy's in the well.
Who put her in?
Little Johnny Green.
Who pulled her out?
Little Tommy Stout.
What a naughty boy was that
To try to drown poor pussy cat,
Who never did him any harm,
But killed all the mice in his father's barn.

## I Had a Little Nut Tree

I had a little nut tree,
   Nothing would it bear
But a silver nutmeg
   And a golden pear;
The king of Spain's daughter
   Came to visit me,
And all for the sake
   Of my little nut tree.

## Pussy Cat

Pussy cat, pussy cat,
   Where have you been?
I've been to London
   To look at the queen.
Pussy cat, pussy cat
   What did you there?
I frightened a little mouse
   Under her chair.

## Ring-a-Ring o' Roses

Ring-a-ring o' roses,
A pocket full of posies,
  A-tishoo! A-tishoo!
We all fall down.

The cows are in the meadow
Lying fast asleep,
  A-tishoo! A-tishoo!
We all get up again.

## Mary's Lamb

Mary had a little lamb,
  Its fleece was white as snow;
And everywhere that Mary went
  The lamb was sure to go.

It followed her to school one day,
  That was against the rule;
It made the children laugh and play
  To see a lamb at school.

And so the teacher turned it out,
  But still it lingered near,
And waited patiently about
  Till Mary did appear.

Why does the lamb love Mary so?
  The eager children cry;
Why, Mary loves the lamb, you know,
  The teacher did reply.

## Baa, Baa, Black Sheep

Baa, baa, black sheep,
  Have you any wool?
Yes, sir, yes, sir,
  Three bags full.
One for the master,
  And one for the dame,
And one for the little boy
  Who lives down the lane.

## The Grand Old Duke of York

Oh, the grand old Duke of York,
    He had ten thousand men;
He marched them up to the top of the hill,
    And he marched them down again.
And when they were up, they were up,
    And when they were down, they were down,
And when they were only halfway up,
    They were neither up nor down.

## Jack and Jill

Jack and Jill
Went up the hill,
To fetch a pail of water;
Jack fell down,
And broke his crown,
And Jill came tumbling after.

Then up Jack got,
And home did trot,
As fast as he could caper,
To old Dame Dob,
Who patched his nob
With vinegar and brown paper.

## Twinkle, Twinkle

Twinkle, twinkle, little star,
How I wonder what you are!
Up above the world so high,
Like a diamond in the sky.

## How Many Miles?

How many miles to Babylon?
Three score and ten.
Will I get there by candlelight?
Yes, and back again.

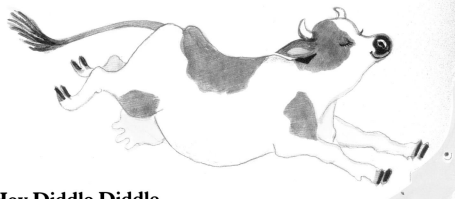

## Hey Diddle Diddle

Hey diddle diddle,
The cat and the fiddle,
    The cow jumped over the moon;
The little dog laughed
To see such sport
    And the dish ran away with the spoon.

# Goodnight Rhyme

Rock-a-bye baby,
Close your eyes tight,
It's time to lie down
And sleep for the night...

Rock-a-bye baby,
This day is done,
Tomorrow is coming,
It's bound to be fun.

Rock-a-bye baby,
Dreams in your head,
There's love all around you –
Sleep safe in your bed!